A GUI

PANSEX

C000157906

NELSON VEGAS

Table of Contents

INTRODUCTION

Since at least the nineteenth century, Americans have associated biological sex with specific sexual behaviors. Sexually assertive and knowledgeable men pursued women. White, upper-class women were sexually submissive.' People were presumed to be heterosexual. We considered variance from the stated sexual norm to be deviant or an illness. Moreover, deviance carried a negative connotation. 8 Today, stereotypes about men and women persist in attributing particular behaviors and characteristics to different biological sexes. Advances in the behavioral and biological sciences have contributed important information regarding the diversity of human sexuality.' While stereotypes persist, most scientists acknowledge, and many people understand, that not all behaviors formerly labeled deviant are abnormal." Homosexuality and bisexuality, despite the protests of religious adherents, are evolving slowly, and in some regions have evolved based on descriptions of sick deviance into categories of accepted sexual difference. Greater acceptance and exploration of these categories, however, demonstrate that many people cannot be pigeonholed into these subcategories.

Heterosexuality, homosexuality, and bisexuality track only the biological sex of the actors in a relationship, as defined by sexual desire. These subcategories fail to describe adequately the panoply of human sexual behavior. First, they fail to describe sexual desire in persons, such as my former client, for whom biological sex is in transition. Second, they fail to describe sexual bonding or dominance behaviors that may not be motivated by sexual desire. For example, some fraternity brothers engage in sexualized rituals during hazing. Are they sexual deviants? Some male heterosexuals rape men in prisons. Are these rapists really homosexual, or even bisexual? The relaxation of societal penalties for cross-category behaviors has allowed people like author Carren Strock, a woman married to a man, to announce that she is a lesbian. Popular movies like Chasing Amy 6 explore the tenuous boundaries between heterosexual and homosexual self-identification and suggest that bisexuality (and perhaps pansexuality) is more prevalent in our society than acknowledged.

Medical advances have made it possible for people like my former client to transform their physical identity to match their self-identified gender. Trans men and women, intersexuals, and hermaphrodites" clearly demonstrate that biological sex does not strictly correlate with gender and sexual behavior.' The terms heterosexual, homosexual, and bisexual define behavior in ways that fail to describe adequately the variety of human sexual experiences currently recognized as "normal" for particular categories of people. Pansexuality' encompasses all kinds of sexuality. It differs, however, from pansexualism, a perspective that declares "all desire and interest are derived from the sex instinct." Pansexuality includes heterosexuality, homosexuality, bisexuality, and sexual behavior that does not necessarily involve a coupling. It includes, for example, masturbation, celibacy, fetishism, and fantasy. Moreover, pansexuality includes heteroerotic and homoerotic play, including sexual aggression, sometimes mislabeled as "horseplay." I submit we are all pansexual, individually, and as a collective. Each individual has the ability to manifest more than one form of sexuality.

Because pansexuality includes sexual fantasizing and masturbation, as well as heterosexual or homosexual coupling activity, many individuals who formerly might have fallen into one category now fit into two or more categories. Consider, for example, a woman who regularly has sexual relations with her husband and also occasionally fantasizes about women when she has sex with her husband or when she masturbates. Or, consider a man who formerly had sex with women only and has had only male partners for the last ten years, but still occasionally fantasizes about women. Commercial advertising patterns and the Internet both support the notion that we are individually and collectively pansexual. Glamorous women sell women everything, from clothing to cars. It is possible that those sexy Victoria's Secret spokeswomen, who usually do not talk much model luxurious underwear. It is also possible that they are "seducing" women into a purchase. Voluptuous Xena, Warrior Princess, and her sexy young apprentice, Gabrielle, sell television advertising time to heterosexual men and women. Androgynous nudes sell perfume to men and women. In addition, by offering the option of anonymity, cyberspace liberates shy pansexuals and allows them to explore, via the Internet, their own sexuality." An Altavista search of the word "pansexual" currently produces 1554 web site hits.

Some individuals, who engage sexually with only one other person, may never fantasize or masturbate. Even those persons, however, may be pansexuals with moral codes that tolerate only one type of expression or behavior. For example, a priest might once have been a heterosexual who fantasized and masturbated. Even if he chooses a life of celibacy, that priest is still a pansexual whose vows constrain his sexual expression. This example highlights that individual sexuality, like religious conviction and practice, can change and evolve. Pansexuality enabled my former client to identify herself as a sexual person without having to pigeonhole herself into a more specifically defined subset. Additionally', she avoided the term "queer" which many people consider a derisive label or one that separates those who are "queer" from those who are "straight." The beauty of pansexuality is that everyone is a member of the pansexual community with a position and dignity equal to that of all other people.

CHAPTER 1
WHAT EXACTLY IS PANSEXUALITY?

More and more celebrities are defining themselves as pansexual. Miley Cyrus and Asia Kate Dillon have embraced the label for years, but recently celebrities have given pansexuality renewed attention, and thus people are wondering, "just what exactly is pansexuality?"

In an inspirational Rolling Stone interview earlier this year, eclectic Indie R&B singer Janelle Monae came out as both queer and pansexual. "I consider myself to be a free-ass motherfucker," said the 32-year-old.

After the interview went viral, lookups of the

word pansexual on Merriam Webster rose 11,000% and the term became the most searched word of the day.

And just days after donating $1 million to LGBT youth under the GLSEN foundation, Panic! at the Disco's Brendon Urie defined his sexuality for PAPER.

"I'm married to a woman and I'm very much in love with her, but I'm not opposed to a man because to me, I like a person." Urie went on, "Yeah, I guess you could qualify me as pansexual because I really don't care."

But What Exactly Is Pansexuality?

The word entered the English language in 1917, although it originally described "the view that the sex instinct plays the primary part in all human activity, mental and physical." Many 20th century critics believed it to be the views of Sigmund Freud and was considered a term of reproach.

Nowadays, it is more commonly understood as a sexual, romantic, or emotional attraction towards a person regardless of their gender identity or orientation. Pansexuals can be attracted to cisgender, transgender, intersex, and androgynous people, so the gender binary is less important and feelings are based on who a person truly is and less on the physical.

In April, Janelle told Rolling Stone about her pansexuality. "Being a queer black woman in America, someone who has been in relationships with both men and women—I consider myself to be a free-ass motherfu#ker," she said. Janelle says she originally identified as bisexual, but realized that label did no't *q*uite fit. "Later I read about pansexuality and was like, 'Oh, these are things that I identify with too,'" she said. "I'm open to learning more about who I am."

Miley had a similar journey to pansexuality. In 2016, she told Variety that she had a hard time understanding her own gender and sexuality. "I always hated the word 'bisexual' because that's even putting me in a box," she explained in the interview. "I don't ever think about someone being a boy or someone being a girl...My eyes started opening in the fifth or sixth grade. My first relationship in my life was with a chick."

Then in a recent interview with Billboard, Miley opened up a bit more about her status as a pansexual: "Who I'm with has nothing to do with sex," she said. "I'm super-open, pansexual, that's just me."

CHAPTER 2
THE TRUTH ABOUT PANSEXUALITY

It is not equivalent to bisexuality, because it 's broader in scope.

Pansexuality as a concept that goes back to the time of Freud, but has achieved new currency as celebrities and an increasing number of millennial youth have claimed a pansexual identity (Grinberg). Whether it connotes a sexual/romantic orientation in addition to an identity is unclear; who is pansexual rests on a proverbial slippery slope.

Pansexual could refer to someone who is sexually and/or romantically attracted to a person regardless of that person's biological sex — It is not their biological e*q*uipment that is most critical. Sociologist Emily Lenning expanded this definition by centrally including gender. Hence, pansexuality is "a sexual attraction to all people, regardless of their gender identity or biological sex." Other sociologists extend even this broad definition by delineating pansexuality as being not about the sexual e*q*uipment of the individual or how feminine or masculine the individual is or feels (gender identity), but about the person as an individual — inclusive of just about anything.

As a working definition, though, most researchers would follow Morandini and colleagues:

"Pansexual is often conceptualized as a label that denotes sexual or romantic attraction to people regardless of their gender expression (masculinity or femininity), gender identity, or biological sex."

They reported that among nonheterosexual pansexual individuals, five times more women than men identified as pansexual. Also, more likely to identify as pansexual were nonheterosexuals from younger generations and those who have a gender identity, gender expression, or gender role that society considers inappropriate for the sex one was assigned at birth (aka "noncisgender"). Finally, pansexual individuals "overwhelmingly represented their sexual/romantic attractions as falling within the bisexual range of the sexual continuum."

This last point has been problematic for many, including the singer/actress Miley Cyrus, who recently came out as pansexual. In a 2016 interview with Variety, she said:

"I always hated the word 'bisexual,' because that's even putting me in a box. I don't ever think about someone being a boy or someone being a girl... My eyes started opening in the fifth or sixth grade. My first relationship in my life was with a chick... I saw one human in particular who didn't identify as male or female. Looking at them, they were both: beautiful and sexy and tough but vulnerable and feminine but masculine. And I related to that person more than I related to anyone in my life."

I agree that we should be very careful to distinguish pansexual from bisexual individuals, even though many pansexuals have "bisexual" attractions and behaviors. However, as Morandini and colleagues pointed out, pansexuality per se "explicitly rejects attractions based on binary notions of sex (male versus female) and gender (man versus woman)." Lenning noted, "Whereas bisexuality implies a dichotomy, pansexuality suggests the possibility of attraction to a spectrum of gender identities."

In addition, there are also many individuals who are exclusively or mostly straight or gay in terms of their sexual orientation who also identify as pansexual. They and others who are in the middle sexualities of the sexual continuum stress additional aspects of the person — such as their personality, temperament, likeability, or body type.

Here are four young men who I have interviewed and who identify themselves as pansexual — note their emphasis on "the person" and on their own fluidity:

Charles, 18: "Sort of don't think of myself as straight or as only attracted to girls. Don't think of myself as gay or bisexual, but just attracted to all people the same. Attracted to the person and not the gender. Nothing to do with them being male or female."

Marcos, 19: "Gender is not an issue. It is the person, the personality."

Dave, 23: "Pansexual because [it depends on the person. I tell people I'm bisexual, but I like girls more, and that I'm sexually attracted to guys, but more into girls, because I find more qualities that I like and find sexually attractive."

Kenworthy, 23: "Pansexual. It's easier to say than bisexual. It depends on the situation. I might say straight…Whatever is true to go with sexual attractions and infatuations at the moment."

The reality is that we actually know little about pansexuals and pansexuality. For example, we do not even know the prevalence of pansexuals, largely because "pansexual" is seldom offered as an option in research studies. We also do nbot know pansexuals' developmental milestones, sexual and romantic histories, personality characteristics, variations among sociodemographic variables, such as race/ethnicity or social class, or even societal attitudes and beliefs about pansexuals.

This is unfortunate, because pansexuality is a real thing with repercussions and importance among millennial youth who are searching for identities that adequately reflect their sexual orientation. Pansexuality offers teenagers an opportunity not to rule out anyone solely because of their sex or gender (Papisova). It explores and even goes beyond traditional categorical identities, such as straight, bisexual, and gay.

CHAPTER 3
THINGS YOU NEED TO KNOW ABOUT PANSEXUALITY

1.It's a real thing.

"There are a lot of stereotypes and misconceptions about pansexuality, and one of the most prominent ones is that pansexuality does not exist, or is not a 'real' sexual identity. "This is absolutely false," says Corey Flanders, Ph.D., an associate professor of psychology and education at Mount Holyoke College. "If a pansexual's sexual identity is denied by others or they're prevented from accepting their own identity, it can stifle them to a certain degree," she says.

2. Pansexual is not the same as bisexual.

Pansexual: Attracted emotionally, romantically, and/or sexually to people of all genders and sexes.

"'Pan' comes for the Greek word 'all'," says Holly Richmond, Ph.D., a certified sex therapist and marriage and family counselor. "Pansexual is not bi-sexual, it's all sexual." That means a pansexual person could be attracted to a man, woman, a transgendered person, or a non-gendered person (a person who chooses not to identify themselves by gender), Richmond says.

3. It is not uncommon for people who once identified as bisexual to become pansexual.

Like Miley and Janelle, some people who formerly identified as bisexual later identify as pansexual. "Bisexuality as a term has experienced criticism for adhering to a binary system of gender, a.k.a. "I'm attracted to men and women,' even though this strict definition of bisexuality doesn't fit many bisexual-identified folks," says Rena McDaniel, who has a master's degree in counseling with a specialty in gender and sexual identity.

Pansexuality, on the other hand, is seen as "more inclusive" of people who are transgender or identify outside of the gender binary of man or woman, she says.

4. Younger generations are more likely to

identify as pansexual.

There seems to be an age gap with this label. McDaniel finds that "younger people are more likely to use pansexual as a term, while slightly older populations are more likely to use bisexual,".n

5. Pansexuality doe not translate to promiscuity.

"Pansexuals may be attracted to all people, but that does not mean that they are going to have sex with anyone", Richmond says. "Pansexuals can be very choosy," she says.

6. Pansexuals want relationships, too.

"One of the ways society shames those who are attracted to more than one gender is to say that they are 'greedy' or a 'commitment-phobe,'" McDaniel says. "However, no one says this about heterosexual folks who also have about half the population of the world to choose from."

"Being attracted to more people has nothing to do with the kind of relationship a person wants to have with their partner or partners," she adds.

7. The term pansexuality has only recently emergedce.

Richmond says that she first started to learn about pansexuality five or six years ago at a conference for the American Association of Sexuality Educators, Counselors, and Therapists. Although pansexual people have definitely been around longer than that, the general public is just starting to acknowledge the term and learn what sexual identity means.

8. Pansexuality has nothing to do with gender.

People often mix up gender identity and sexual identity but they are not the same. "Pansexuality is a term that refers to sexual orientation, who someone is attracted to," McDaniel says. "It is completely different from gender identity, which refers to how someone identifies their own gender."

So pansexuality is not the same as transgender or gender non-binarye. Using pansexual as a label for your sexual orientation does not say anything about your gender identity or the gender identity of the person you are into, she argues.

9. Less than 1 percent of the population identifies as pansexual.

Because pansexuality is a fairly new concept to many people, it is hard to pinpoint exactly how many identify with the label, according to Richmond. She puts her best estimate at less than 1 percent. But as more people become aware of pansexuality, there may be more people who come to identify that way, she says.

10. Pansexuality is not just about sex.

When pansexuals are making a romantic connection, it is very much about connecting with the person—not the gender, Richmond says. "It's about developing meaningful relationships."

So, are pansexuals attracted to absolutely

everyone?

Of course, pansexuals can still have preferences, as they are not attracted to every single person in the world. In Zoë's case, she has a preference for "soft nerd boys" when it comes to men, but more often than not she finds other trans women more compatible because of how they understand her gender, what it is like to experience gender dysphoria, and how queer trauma impacts her everyday life.

In other words, pansexuals like my girlfriend have the ability to feel sexual and romantic attraction to people throughout the gender spectrum, including those that do not identify with a gender at all. It is the individual characteristics that shine through for pan people, and gender is not inherently a roadblock to bonding with others.

"I look for a real connection with a partner," Zoë told me. "I'm a bit of a niche person, and it takes a niche person to get me. When I feel that connection, it just clicks. Someone's gender doesn't influence how I feel about them. Their character does. That being said, historically I've found that trans women tend to understand me a bit better. Cis men have made for decent sexual encounters, but not much more."

How big is the pansexual population?

It i's hard to say for certain how big the pan population is. While pansexuality is largely embraced within the LGBTQ letters under the queer umbrella, the identity often remains relegated to the sidelines while binary depictions of sexuality, such as homosexuality or bisexuality, are given relatively more representation.

However, just like other queer identities, it is certainly likely that the pansexual population is not that large. A May 2018 Gallup poll estimates that the total LGBTQ population in the U.S. was 4.5 percent in 2017. A GLAAD and Harris Poll study from 2017 also reported that pansexual identification remains low throughout age groups: Two percent of millennials identify as pansexual, and only one percent of gen x, baby boomers, and the silent generation consider themselves pan.

That does not necessarily mean that pansexuality is rare. Just as Gallup has reported higher LGBTQ populations across the U.S. over the past decade, it is likely that the pansexual population will increase as pansexuality awareness, representation, and acceptance grows, too. That seems likely based on the fact that millennials are more likely to identify as pansexual than older generations, although for now, the data we have on file does not shed a lot of light onto pan demographic numbers.

Is pansexuality just another label?

No, I really do not think so. In fact, I think it is important to put a name to the feeling. Previous to last year, I did not even know what pansexuality was. I struggled with my sexuality and felt out of place when calling myself something I was not. It was not until college that I realized that maybe I was not so alone. But I wondered, if I felt this way, how many other people have struggled to find their place in the LGBTQ+ community?

The word pansexual has been around for

ages, but it was not until recent years that it took its place on the spectrum. It was first used by Sigmund Freud to describe the sexual desires of humans; however, he never really coined the term as a sexual orientation. Pansexuality as an orientation really took off at the end of the 20th century, leading into the 21st century. So why then do so few people know about it? And how can we make pansexuality a term that is readily available to younger generations?

For me, pansexuality is much more than just my sexual orientation. It has helped me to put into perspective my behavior toward all people.

If you or someone you know is questioning their sexuality, I think it is incredibly important to look all aspects of the LGBTQ+

community. There are so many orientations, genders, and identities that are not covered in schools or by acronyms that deserve to be discussed. Personally, I went to a high school that did not do much to explain anything other than the heteronormative in health class. I think it will take time to implement more LGBTQ+-friendly curriculum into schools; however, I think that clubs, events, and open discussions are a wonderful way to expand queer vocabulary. If words like demisexual, asexual, queer, intersex, nonbinary, etc. are talked about more frequently, it will allow those who are unsure a chance to interact with others who feel like them.

CHAPTER 4
DIFFERENCES BETWEEN BISEXUAL AND PANSEXUAL.

There is some overlap when defining bisexual and pansexual orientation; however, there are important differences between the two identities.

Bisexual people are attracted sexually and romantically to both males and females, and are capable of engaging in sensual relationships with either sex. Despite being able to form meaningful, lasting relationships with both sexes, bisexual individuals may, to a small or large degree, have a preference for one sex over the other.

Similarly, pansexual people may be sexually attracted to individuals who identify as male or female; however, they may also be attracted to those who identify as intersex, third-gender, androgynous, transsexual, or the many other sexual and gender identities.

The latter distinction is what draws the line between pansexuality and bisexuality. People who self-identify as pansexual do so with purpose because they want, to express their ability to be attracted to various genders and sexual identities, whether they fall within the gender binary or not.

Recognition of the existence of different genders and sexualities is a major aspect of pansexual identity. Pansexual people are bisexual; in-fact, however, bisexuality does not place the same emphasis on sexual and gender identity awareness, but more simply indicates attraction to the two (generally accepted) biological sexes.

The differences between the two sexual identities are undermined by the fact that some people who consider themselves pansexual identify themselves as bisexual out of convenience, as it is a more widely known sexual identity. In addition, some people who consider themselves bisexual may be open to dating someone who falls outside the gender binary.

Self-perception, rather than objective sexuality, determines which sexual identity an individual chooses to embrace. Simply being attracted to both biological sexes does not mean one considers oneself bisexual. In fact, many people at one time or another will have some romantic or sexual experience or feelings toward each sex, though, most would not embrace the bisexual label. Similarly, being attracted to people who embrace varied identities does not mean that an individual will identify himself or herself as pansexual.

There are few organizations which are geared solely for those who identify as pansexual, and many bisexual organizations include alternative identities such as: pansexual, omnisexual, multisexual, and other non-monosexualities, so representation and visibility likely also play a part in how people choose to identify.

There is some controversy over the two labels, as some in the bisexual community feel as though the pansexual label is a form of bisexual erasure and that the bisexual identity is already inclusive of those who have an attraction to those who fall anywhere along the gender continuum and outside of it.

There is a feeling that pansexual people are simply avoiding the bisexual label due to the stigmas associated with it (that bisexual people are simply greedy and promiscuous, and spread disease among both the heterosexual and homosexual communities). Conversely, many in the pansexual community feel as though these beliefs are forms of prejudice and pansexual erasure.

Not only those who identify as biologically male or female identify as bisexual, the gender identities of people who use and feel comfortable with this label vary.

The pansexual label; however, is more accommodating for those, regardless of their own gender identity, who sometimes do not fit neatly into the male or female genders, for example, when people who are engaged in a homosexual or heterosexual relationship and their partner transitions from male-to-female or female-to-male. Although, some choose to change their sexual identity according to the gender to which their partner has transitioned, an increasing number have chosen to self-label as pansexual, queere, or one of the other non-monosexual identities.

The pansexual identity is much more accommodating to the coupling of individuals who embrace various sexual and gender identities.

Many people strongly identify as either bisexual or pansexual, and never use the labels interchangeably. Each community is represented by its own flag, set of colors, and general ideologies.

Bisexuality, pansexuality, sexually fluid, queer and simply "not doing labels" – all are different ways people identify to indicate that they are not exclusively attracted to either men or women. The truth is, however, there is confusion even among members of the LGBTQ community as to what these words mean, particularly when it comes to bisexuality. In fact, the bisexual community does not even agree on what it means to be bisexual. The term pansexual was birthed out of the confusion and to create a definitive and more inclusive label. This has led to in-fighting between members of the community who are upset that their bisexual identity is being replaced by another label.

The meaning of pansexual is clear: someone who is attracted – either emotionally, physically, or both – to all genders. This includes cisgender, transgender, agender, and gender nonconforming individuals. The prefix was chosen because it comes from the Greek root "pan", meaning "all." But that is obviously not the case. Two months ago, when Janelle Monáe came out as queer and pansexual in a Rolling Stone cover story, searches for the word pansexual on Merriam Webster rose 11,000 percent, and the term became the most looked up word of the day.

The prefix "bi," as we are all aware, means two. Because of this, many folks, perhaps even the majority of people, believe that a bisexual person is attracted to only two genders: cisgender men and cisgender women. Members of the queer community who believe this to be the definition of bisexual, believe that bisexuality perpetuates a gender binary. They do not believe it is inclusive of transgender people and gender nonconforming people.

Given that "bi" means two, that is a reasonable belief.

However, many bisexual-identifying individuals, myself included, now use renowned bisexual activist Robyn Och's definition of bisexuality, as stated on her website: "I call myself bisexual because I acknowledge that I have in myself the potential to be attracted – romantically and/or sexually – to people of more than one sex and/or gender, not necessarily at the same time, not necessarily in the same way, and not necessarily to the same degree."

In this definition, the "bi" stands for two (or more) genders. Gabrielle Blonder, a board member of the Bisexual Resource Center, a nonprofit whose mission is "providing support to the bisexual community and raising public awareness about bisexuality and bisexual people," explains, "I use it to mean 'attracted to genders like mine and genders different from mine.'"

The majority of pansexual individuals do not believe either of these definitions – and that is precisely why they prefer the term pansexual.

When the word "bisexual" became popularized, starting with David Bowie when he claimed bisexuality in a Playboy interview in 1976, we did not have a nuanced understanding of gender like we do today. Now that we do have a better understanding, some bisexual people have updated the definition of bisexual to be inclusive of all genders, whereas others have favored abandoning it, for a new word, that frankly is less confusing, given that pan does indeed mean "all."

Some pansexual folks even go a step further. "There's the argument to be had that people use all the time, that bi is exclusionary. It feeds into the binary of gender," says Tortella. "And

I know that for me personally, that's not the case. A lot of people say that bi is trans-exclusionary, but trans is not a gender itself, it's a descriptor word for how people express their gender."

That's why Ethan Remillard, 22, who came out as bisexual in his early teens, said bluntly, "I identify as bisexual because I like fucking dudes and romancing girls. But I don't claim pansexuality because trans[gender] girls and boys are the same as their cis[gender] counterparts."

This is partly why people do not like identifying with any sexual or gender identity label. Simply put, it is confusing, and for many, the labels feels limiting. Also, inherent in your sexuality is an understanding of your own gender. If you are not completely sure if you identify as male or female, then how can you accurately state your own sexuality?

This contributes to the growing popularity of the reclaimed word, "queer".

"I use the term queere because I'm not sure

of the specifics of my gender identity," says Jill B., a 23-year-old artist. "So 'queer' feels like a good umbrella placeholder while I grow and learn and figure out all the details."

People also have no qualms claiming multiple sexual identity labels. "Early on in my coming out, bisexual just fit ... and queer felt disconnected from who I was, a bit academic and drudged in hate," says Ryan Carey-Mahoney, 26, a LGBTQ activist. "Then, as I grew into myself a bit more, I found queer to be none of those things. It was inclusive of many identities – bisexuality and others – and brought people together. It was uniting in a way that just saying 'gay' when describing the community can feel dividing."

Now, Carey-Mahoney identifies with both labels. "They both, now, fit me like a glove, and trust me, honey, I'm wearing them proudly."

Interestingly, when Tortorella does wish to identify with sexual labels – as opposed to simply human – he actively changes his label depending on who he is speaking to and what their intention is.

"If I'm talking to somebody who's more conservative and doesn't believe in a nonbinary gender, then it's easier to use the word bisexual, but if I'm talking to someone who's invested in gender, queer theory, and understands the spectrum, then I'm more comfortable using the word 'pansexual' or the word 'fluid.'"

Fluid, in this case, meaning that sexual attractions have the capacity to change over time and can be dependent on different situations.

Tortella does note, however, that there is a rich history to the word bisexual, and it would be nice to honor it.

"The B existed far longer than the P ever did in the acronym, and there's something to be said about that," he says. "There's something to be said about standing up for the mothers and fathers of the community who fought for [our rights to embrace a queer identity]."

Tortella's not alone in his reasoning. "I personally like the historical aspect of it," says BRC's Blonder. "It's the label we've fought for recognition under for decades, and it's the most widely-known label. Language isn't a static entity, and words can change meaning over time. Much like October is no longer the eighth month of the year, I believe the term bisexual has morphed into a different meaning than it originally was."

For others, it is less about history and more about the arduous, personal journey it took to finally claim a sexual label, only to then be told that their label is wrong, obsolete, or transphobic – and by members of the same community who are supposed to be embracing them no less.

"I'm proud to be bisexual" says Daniel Saynt, founder of NSFW, a private club offering educational experiences in relationships, kink and intimacy. "It took me 30 years to get to that point and it sucks that now that I'm comfortable in my sexuality, I'm told I'm not accepting enough cause I don't consider myself pansexual. Pansexuals shouldn't be attacking bisexuals just cause there's a new term that's more inclusive. We don't attack gays for not being attracted to women and we shouldn't attack a bisexual [person] just because they may not find a trans person attractive."

Saynt is one of the people for whom bisexuality does indeed mean exclusively attracted to cisgender men and women. He embodies what many bisexual activists and individuals are fighting against.

"I've definitely met attractive trans and non-conforming individuals, but the feelings I have [for them have] never been sexual in nature," Saynt continues. "It's more of an appreciation for who they are, what they represent, and just a desire for them to find happiness regardless of identity."

The question then becomes, is it transphobic to not be attracted to transgender and gender non-conforming individuals? If so, then are members of the LGBTQ community clinging to a label that is potentially harmful to other members of the LGBTQ community?

"For some time, I felt compelled to cling to the bisexual label in a pseudo-noble effort to protect the identity from a perceived diaspora of individuals turning to the term pansexual," Jill B. says. "At first, it felt important to continue defending bisexuality, as I had always done when members of the straight or gay communities attempted to invalidate or exclude it. [I felt] like a captain going down with his ship. Over time, this came to be less important than accurately portraying the full spectrum of my sexuality."

Nevertheless, everyone I spoke to said that there is room in the larger bi and pansexual communities for multiple labels to exist.

"I think there's room for all of. We're all here. And it's our right to claim whichever label we want." Tortorella said.

Bisexuality, to many, is also seen as an umbrella term, inclusive of sexually fluid labels like pansexual. There is even been a push in the bisexual community to use the term bi+ to really emphasize that bisexuality is the larger encompassing term.

Jill B., even though they abandoned the bi label, still believes there is room in the queer community for the diversity of sexually fluid labels. "I'm hopeful that the spark in conversation regarding sexual fluidity will generally increase visibility for those who neither fully identify as straight or gay."

Still, they are not convinced if having all these labels will be beneficial to the community in the long run. As Jill B. notes, "I am not sure whether an increase in labels will prove to be unifying or divisive for us."

CHAPTER 5

WHAT ARE THE SEXUAL ORIENTATIONS OF THOSE WHO IDENTIFY AS QUEER OR PANSEXUAL?

One basic yet unanswered *q*uestion relates to the sexualorientation of nonheterosexuals who gravitate toward pansexualor queer labels. That is, are these individuals predominantlymonosexual (i.e., attracted to one gender) or nonmonosexual (i.e., attracted to more than one gender), or do substantialproportions of both monosexual and nonmonosexual individuals adopt these labels? To address this question, we first need to distinguish what is meant by sexual identity versus sexual orientation. Sexual identity refers to a label adopted by an individual to communicate the most salient aspect of his or her sexuality (Savin-Williams, 2011). Traditionally, this relates to sexual orientation and conforms to the social categories of lesbian/gay, bisexual, or straight. As discussed, there is evidence that individuals are increasingly adopting sexual identities which not only refer to sexual orientations but also encompass other aspects of their sexuality, including attraction to personal characteristics regardless of gender (e.g., sapiosexual), sexual attraction only in the context of a romantic bond (e.g., demisex-ual or graysexual), preference for particular sexual activities orrelationship types (e.g., kink or polyamorist) (Savin-Williams,2011), as well as queer and pansexual. Sexual orientation typically refers to an individual's tendency to experience sexual attraction, arousal, desire, and fantasy toward men, women, or both, to varying degrees.

There is a general consensus that male sexual orientation is relatively stable across the life course and that it is specific   category. Typically, men experience sexual desire toward either women or men, with bisexual sexualdesires comparatively rare. By contrast, female sexual orientation appears more fluid, meaning that the target of women's sexual desires or romantic infatuations may change over time. Moreover,women tend to report less exclusivity in facets of their sexual orientation. For instance, compared with men, women are more likely to report bisexual sexual desires than they are to report exclusive same-sex desires. It is typically thought that sexual orientation determines not only the gender we sexually desire but also the gender with whom we fall in love. Evidence suggests, however, that while sexual and romantic attractions align for mostpeople, they may function somewhat independently for others. These experiences fit with emerging theoretical perspectives on the distinction between sexual desire and love, which propose that while sexual desire is inherently oriented to a particular sex, romantic love is not. In fact, there is evidence that some sexual minority individuals distinguish between their sexual versus romantic orientations, even integrating these distinctions into their sexual identities, with distinct labels for sexual versus romantic dispositions (e.g., homosexualpanromantic).

Accordingly, recent studies emphasize the importance of measuring sexual and romantic attraction when assessing sexual orientation in contemporary samples of nonhetero-sexuals, given that both sexual and romantic attractions may influence how individuals conceptualize their sexual identity. Distinct from these constructs is sexual behavior pattern, which relates to with whom (e.g., same sex, other sex, or both) one has sex. In addition to one's sexual orientation (who one sexually desires), sexual behavior pattern may be influenced by factors, such as availability of potential partners and the presence of negative societal attitudes (andeven legal prohibitions) toward same-sex sexuality. Indeed, in some instances, bisexual or lesbian/gay individuals mayforgo same-sex relationships and/or sexual encounters to avoid stigma. Keeping these distinctions in mind, what types of non-heterosexual individuals adopt queer or pansexual sexualidentities? It stands to reason that queer and pansexuallabels are most frequently adopted by those who experience sexual attraction to more than one gender (i.e. non-monosexuals). In this case, queer and pansexual populations would be similar insexual/romantic attraction and sexual behavior to those who are bisexual identified with their differences having more to do with their sexual politics than their sexual orientation per se. Moreover, some nonmonosexual indi-viduals may adopt queer and pansexual labels to avoid stigma associated with a bisexual identity.

However, if queer and pansexual labels reflect elements beyond just a renaming of the stigmatized label bisexual, an investigation of the distinguishing characteristics of the individuals who adopt these labels is warranted. For instance, it is plausible, that some queer-identified individuals are homo-sexual (sexual orientation) and publicly identify as queer forpolitical reasons, such as a commitment to progressive notions of gender and sexuality. A further question is whether the likelihood of adopting queer and pansexual identities differs by sex and gender identity. As bisexual attraction is morecommon than exclusive same-sex attraction in women (and given that the reverse is true for men), queer and pansexualidentities are therefore expected to be more prevalent in women than men. In addition, as conceptualizing and labeling one's sexual identity may be more complex for noncisgender individuals (e.g., traditional sexual identities may come withunwanted assumptions about one's gender), noncisgender individuals may also be more likely to adopt queer and pansexualidentities than cisgender individuals, as suggested by previous research (Katz-Wise et al., 2015). Empirical data are thereforere quired to shed light on the sexual orientations and gender identities of those who adopt queer and pansexual identities incontemporary sexual minority populations.

CHAPTER 6
10 WAYS TO KNOW IF YOU ARE PANSEXUAL OR BISEXUAL

Coming to terms with your own sexual orientation can be a confusing and difficult experience. If you grew up in a place where the LGBT+ community is not accepted, you may be afraid to admit to yourself that you are not straight. Likewise, if you have always thought of yourself as a gay man or a lesbian, it may be confusing to you if you suddenly find yourself attracted to a member of your non-preferred gender. Though many people look at sexual orientation as a black and white, either/or identity and assume most people must be either attracted to men or to women, human sexuality actually exists on a spectrum, so it is very likely you are not 100% straight or 100% gay. Here are some ways to help you figure out if you are actually bi, pan, or otherwise non-monosexual.

You Are Attracted to Guys and Girls

This is the most obvious sign that you are bi or pan. You probably are not mono-sexual if you sometimes find yourself staring a little too long at cute guys and girls. If you find yourself physically attracted to men and women, or even people who identify outside of the male/female gender binary, you are probably bi or pan. Perhaps you have developed crushes on friends and celebrities of different genders.

You Fantasize About Your Own Gender

You prefer to watch adult videos or read steamy stories featuring your own gender only, even if you sometimes also enjoy straight intimate content. If you find yourself fantasizing about being with someone of your own gender, chances are you, on some level, wish to experience it firsthand.

You Felt Relieved When You First Heard the Term "Bisexual"

When you first heard of bisexuality, you immediately felt less alone. Even if you were not yet ready to claim that label for yourself, it might have been a huge weight off your shoulders to find out that there are other people out there who are attracted to multiple genders.

Your "Happily Ever After" Could Go Either Way

When you imagine your future in which you can see yourself with either a man or a woman. You would be just as happy if you end up with a husband as you would be if you end up with a wife. At the end of the day, you just want to be in a happy relationship with someone you love.

Conversely, Your Own Gender Makes You Nervous

You may find yourself pushing people of your own gender away if you are bi or pan, but have not come to terms with your identity yet. This may sound counter-intuitive, but your own gender may make you feel uncomfortable if you are not ready to deal with your attractions. For example, straight women tend to be very comfortable hugging their female friends, but a closeted bi woman may feel uncomfortable hugging other women, subconsciously fearing that they inadvertently out themselves.

You Feel at Home in LGBT+ Spaces

You feel more comfortable and at home with LGBT+ people, even if you have been in relationships that appear "straight" to the outside observer. Sometimes you just feel more at ease with people who have things in common with you, even if you are not ready to admit that about yourself yet.

You Are Attracted to Androgyny

You find yourself attracted to androgynous people, even if you do not know their actual gender identity. Though not all bi and pan people will be attracted to the androgynous look, if you are attracted to someone despite not knowing how they identify, you are likely non-monosexual.

Bisexual Stereotypes Offend You

On the other hand, you are probably also offended when you hear someone imply that all bisexuals are into threesomes, polyamory, or are promiscuous. Maybe you are afraid to call yourself bisexual because you know that these stereotypes do not apply to you.

You Cannot Make Up Your Mind

If you see a cute (male/female) couple, you cannot decide if you think the man or the woman is more attractive. Perhaps you want them both, even if you would never tell them that! You enjoy variety. Maybe you briefly consider whether you would like to try a polyamorous relationship, even if you know deep down that you prefer monog my.

It Just Feels Right

The term "bi" or "pan" just feels right to you. Deep down, you know you are not straight or gay. Even if you are not ready to be out just yet, deep down you know that you are interested in different genders. Take your time exploring your identity, and just be you!

CONCLUSION

So what has my year as an openly pansexual been like? Honestly, I feel like a weight has been lifted off my shoulders. For me, pansexuality is much more than just my sexual orientation. It has helped me to put into perspective my behavior toward all people. Perhaps my heart is just a little too big, but I believe that every person I come across, regardless of gender, race, religion, sexuality, etc., sdeserves some type of connection, whether it be emotional, physical, or intellectual. Those connections are what made me who I am and I think what led me to pansexuality.

I do not think I could have done this without my incredible roommate, who has listened to my struggles for countless hours and encouraged me to explore my sexuality. I a'm also incredibly grateful for my family who are always asking questions and have gone above and beyond to research pansexuality and the LGBTQ+ community.

I am not sure what is in store for me; however, I know now that I am not alone or "confused." In fact, I am the furthest thing from confused. I did not need some big revelation to tell me that I was pansexual. All it really took was some reflection and a Google search.

IMPRINT

Printed in Great Britain
by Amazon